The story of Twirp is based on a real dog whose
previous owner became too ill to take care of her.
The author was helping to find Twirp a new home by writing
a description of her personality (doggie-ality?), and as she added
to the description, a book began to unfold. "My name is Twirp"
tells the happy story of how Twirp and her new Person learn
to adapt to each other and form a new and special bond.

The author, Karen Smith lives and
writes in the Skagit River Valley
in Northwestern Washington State.

The illustrator, Don Smith lives and paints with
his wife Cherie, also an artist, and their dog Stella
and three cats in Rockport, Washington.

© 2016 ISBN # 9781540337320

This story is dedicated to Dog and Library lovers everywhere

As a member of the animal world
I have the grand title of "Man's Best Friend".
I know a lot of words and hand signals.
I instinctively understand human emotions
and that they sometimes have special needs.

People say that I am a "lapdog"

because I am a small dog and that is where I like to sit. The question, "Do you want to be a baby?" will have me running to lay on my back in your lap for hours, just like a little baby. It is quite comfortable for me. I am really a female Pekingese dog. Of course I prefer to think I am more human than other dogs. -I even have a mission to help humans!

The word 'eat' will wake me out of a sound sleep.

...εat.

I have a little mouth and dog food is hard to chew so I like to eat boiled chicken legs, among other things. I have tried every kind of dog food and frankly- it smells like ...dog food.

Sometimes I like to be hand-fed a treat.

Cheese is one of my favorite snacks.
Palms flat to my view means, "all gone!".
If I get anxious around strangers or company
it can also mean that they are "all gone".

Occasionally I need a good S-t-r-e-t-c-h...

I like to go outside to play. It is even more fun when you go with me. I need to go outside to "do my business" too!

The word 'ride' is more fun and even better than the word 'eat' on most occasions!

I will sit still during a bath.
However I would
prefer to get by
without one,
given the choice..

Sometimes I try to hide when
I hear the word "bath", but it usually doesn't work.

"Sit Pretty" - I will do this trick for food if it seems to be important to you. Sometimes it works well when it is my own idea.

"Not Your Business" means that I shouldn't bark
at people passing by my fenced yard.
I am not a "yappy" dog, but I will
give a warning bark to strangers.

I have been taught good manners and most of the time I behave quite well. I know that it is not proper to beg for food,

though I can use my eyes quite effectively to get some of it forked over to me.

To let you know that I am annoyed I will frown while taking my paw and batting it past my eyebrow.

That also means that I don't want to play a game right now.

My "Dumb Bunny Look":
Sometimes I like to act like I don't have a clue what you are talking about. I will roll my eyes toward the top of my head like I am trying to understand what you are saying.
We both know that I know the words!

I will roll over on my back for a belly rub whenever I think it is a good time for one.

You may continue rubbing my belly for as long as you like!

Coloring Pages-

Now you can color Twirp any way you like!

Made in the USA
San Bernardino, CA
22 November 2016